Baby Moo's Great Escape

By Julie Flanders

Native Ink Press

www.nativeinkpress.com

Printed in the United States of America

First Printing, 2016
ISBN 978-1-939156-84-6

Native Ink Press
710 S. Myrtle Ave Suite 209
Monrovia, CA, 91016
www.nativeinkpress.com

Dedicated to all of the beautiful animals who call Sunrise
Sanctuary home

Baby Moo's Great Escape

"Cock-a-doodle-do! Cock-a-doodle-do!"

Mr. Big the rooster alerted everyone at Sunrise Sanctuary that a new day was at hand. For Baby Moo, a young cow with a furry black coat that sometimes made him look a bit like a bear, this day was going to be an exciting one indeed.

Moo used his hoof to close the travel magazine he had been browsing overnight while most of the farm's inhabitants slept. Ruthie, an orange tabby cat who was one of his best friends in the world, had been in the barn that night to keep him company. He was always glad when Ruthie decided to stay in with him instead of heading out on one of her nocturnal strolls around the countryside.

"Missy will be here for that any minute, Moo," Ruthie said, her voice coming out in a purr.

As if on cue, Missy, Moo's other best friend, arrived at that second.

"I need to take the magazine back, Moo. You know I can't be late. Mom can't find out I bring these to you!"

Missy was a brown, black, and white corgi mix with a thick coat and short legs that were out of proportion with the rest of her body. She came from something Moo had heard Mom call a "puppy mill," but Moo didn't understand what that was. He only knew it had left Missy full of anxiety. She was nervous about everyone and everything.

She wore a pink shirt with the words "Wild at Heart" on the back due to her itchy skin, but Missy was anything but wild. She was more cautious than anyone Moo had ever known.

"I know, Missy, I know," he said, shoving the magazine towards her. Missy picked it up with her mouth and disappeared from the barn in a flash. Moo knew she would be as quiet as the barn mice when she returned the magazine to Mom's living room.

Moo loved Missy for bringing him their mom's travel magazines. Because of them, and because of Ruthie's ability to read the articles to him, he'd learned of amazing places like Sydney, Australia, Paris, France, and Rio de Janeiro, Brazil. Moo had been especially intrigued by a picture of the famous Sydney Opera House. He loved to sing, and imagined himself taking center stage there one day. In his dreams he heard the adoring crowd cheering as opened his mouth to sing.

Moo looked at the cross-stitch sign that had hung on the wall of the barn for as long as he'd lived at Sunrise. "Be it ever so humble, there's no place like home," it said. Ruthie had told him the line was from an old song called Home, Sweet Home.

Moo liked the song, and there was no question Sunrise was a sweet place. But he had learned that there was a great big world outside of his home and outside of Marysville, the town the sanctuary called home.

Moo had every intention of exploring it.

*

"So are you still planning to leave today, Moo?" Missy asked as she returned to the barn from the house.

"Yes, I am," Moo said. "Today's the day! I'm making

my escape."

"And just where do you think you're going?" Ruthie asked.

"I don't know. Wherever my hooves take me."

Ruthie stared at him with undisguised disgust. "Moo, you're acting like an idiot."

"Why?"

"Really? You have to ask why?" Missy said. She shook her ears and stretched forward in a yoga position, one of many moves she did to try to relax. It didn't really work.

"Yes!" Moo said, offended. "I want to know why."

"Because you have a good home here."

Moo snorted and kicked some straw with his hoof.

"I did. Until that baby Nathan showed up. He ruined everything."

"Not this again," Ruthie said. She turned her back to Moo and began her morning bath.

Nathan was a piglet who had come to Sunrise after surviving a truck accident. He had been found in the wreckage and eventually found his way to the sanctuary. He was cute and pink and tiny, and everyone loved him. Everyone but Moo.

"Moo, you're just jealous of Nathan." Missy said.

"I am not!"

He absolutely was. Before Nathan's arrival, Moo had been the "baby" of Sunrise. He'd been given toys and treats and even had his own birthday party when he'd turned one.

Everyone who visited wanted to see Baby Moo. But now they all wanted to see Baby Nathan.

"Well whether you are or not, you're stupid!" Missy said, barking at the end to add weight to her declaration. "You have a good life here. And there's lots of bad out there. Maybe you were too young to remember your life before you came here but I remember mine very well. And you're crazy to want to leave Sunrise. Just plain crazy!"

Moo started to respond, but was interrupted by Ruthie, who was licking her paw repeatedly and running it over her face.

"For once the dog is talking sense, Moo. I never thought I'd say this, but she's right. I remember what it was like before I came here too."

Moo knew Ruthie had lived in a place that had way too many cats and dogs before she moved to Sunrise, but he didn't know why it was so bad. Except that Ruthie had told him once that the house was also filled with garbage. He couldn't really imagine a house filled with garbage, but he took Ruthie's word for it. It must have been a nasty place to live.

"Well just because you two had problems doesn't mean I will. I can't help it if don't want to spend my whole life here in Marysville. I just want to see what else is out there! Maybe I could even go to Rio. Or Australia! Imagine that! I could sing at the Sydney Opera House!"

"Oh boy," Missy said. "Is that really what this is about? Your singing career?"

"No it's about seeing the world. But since no one here appreciates my singing maybe people in Australia will."

"Moo, you really need to listen to sense," Ruthie said. "We don't appreciate your singing because you can't sing. I'm sorry but it's the truth."

Moo snorted and stomped the floor of the barn. "I can sing!"

"You can't!" Missy said. "Ruthie is right. You may love doing it but that doesn't mean you're good. If that's why you're leaving here you're even crazier than I thought."

"You guys aren't going to talk me out of this. As soon as we have breakfast and Mom leaves for work I'm leaving. That's all there is to it."

He stomped the floor again to emphasize his point.

Before Missy or Ruthie could respond, they all heard their Mom calling the animals for breakfast. Time for hay for Moo and canned food for Ruthie and Missy. Their argument could wait.

*

Afternoon came and Moo prepared to leave the farm where he'd spent all of the life that he could remember. As he walked towards the gate, Ruthie and Missy walked on either side of him.

"Aren't you going to miss us, Moo?" Missy asked. "We'll miss you."

"Of course I'll miss you. But sometimes a man just has to break out on his own."

"Where did you hear such nonsense?" Ruthie asked. "And when did you decide you were a man? Have you forgotten you're a cow?"

"Well fine, a bull needs to go out on his own then. That okay with you?"

As Moo made his way to the gate, other residents of the sanctuary fell in behind him.

"Looks like everyone is going to miss you, Moo. Everyone's here."

Moo turned around and saw Danny the horse, Chance the dog, Roscoe and Willy the donkeys, Woody and Milly the goats, Teddy the cat, Franco and Vanessa the ducks, Louise and Chester the turkeys, Mr. Big the rooster, Skye the peacock, Ping and Julie the pigs, and all of his other friends getting up from their afternoon naps to say goodbye to him. Even George and Gracie the llamas were there and Moo didn't think they even liked him. He didn't think they liked anyone.

Maybe he was making a mistake…

"We'll miss you, Moo!" a piglet squealed.

Oh, boy. He should have known baby Nathan would show up to steal his thunder even now. Moo supposed he should be glad Nathan did show up. He was the reminder Moo needed that the farm was for babies, not a growing bull like him.

"Thank you all for coming out," he said, facing his friends. "I'll miss you all."

"Where are you headed, Moo?" Danny asked.

"Not sure. Wherever my hooves take me, I guess."

Moo turned back towards the gate and easily lifted the latch he had learned to open weeks earlier. Most of the animals knew how to open it, but all kept that fact a secret from their mom. No one but Moo wanted to open it anyway. He was the only one who wanted to escape.

It was strange to have the gate open without Mom around though. Moo hesitated, doubting himself for a second or two. But then he thought of all the places he'd seen in the magazines. All the places he wanted to see. He walked out of the gate and down the drive towards the main road. Missy and Ruthie continued to follow him.

A beat-up truck pulling a horse trailer behind it came puttering down the road and stopped at the Sunrise driveway. A man wearing boots and a cowboy hat got out and looked at Moo. He had a protruding belly that his grey shirt barely covered. The man had a fat red face that was wet with sweat even though the day was cool. His hair matched the color of his face, and a handlebar mustache curled around his thin lips. His eyes were small and squinty, and he looked at Moo with a grin that exposed pointed yellow teeth. Ruthie was sure she'd seen this truck and its driver before. He made a habit of cruising past the farm whenever mom wasn't home. Ruthie didn't like him.

"Going somewhere, fella?" the man asked Moo.

"Don't answer him," Ruthie hissed. "He's up to no good."

"Oh, Ruthie, you think that about everyone."

Ruthie arched her back in an attempt to warn the driver away. She made her tail as fat as it would get and stood on her toes. Missy, who always believed in Ruthie's judgement, joined in, barking and growling at the driver as Moo walked ever closer to him.

"He's going to take him to be sold," Ruthie whispered. "He'll bring him to an auction!"

Missy didn't really know what an auction was, but she was terrified just the same. She stepped up her barking and ran towards the driver, who now had his hand on Moo's bridle.

Missy nipped at the man's boots and jumped at his thick legs, growling and showing her fangs.

"Hey now little wild at heart," the man said, reading Missy's t-shirt. "You need to get control of yourself, dog."

Missy barked and lunged at the man, biting his jeans. She hoped she got some of his leg too, and was satisfied she had when he yowled and cursed at the sky.

"I told you to control yourself, you mutt!"

With that, he kicked her with his boot, sending her tumbling backwards onto the gravel of the driveway.

Moo, his brown eyes wide with horror at the injury to his friend, tried to pull away from the red-faced man. But the man's grip was too tight, and he forced a now kicking and stomping Moo through the door of the horse trailer.

Ruthie made a last ditch effort, running at the man and jumping onto his chest. She dug in her claws and scratched her way down his torso. Blood sprinkled his grey shirt with red.

"Now a cat!" the man yelled, kicking Ruthie in the same direction he had Missy. "What kind of crazy animals are you?"

He stomped his feet and ran towards Missy and Ruthie, threatening both with more kicks. The other animals began to whinny and bark and bleat and squeal from the other side of the gate. Danny the horse stood up on his back legs and neighed as loud as he could.

The man stood back, clearly intimidated by the size and fury of the horse. "What's the matter with all of ya?" he yelled. He ran towards the gate, waving his big arms and howling with rage. "Get back! Every last one of you, get back now!"

Before returning to his truck, he kicked both Ruthie and Missy again for good measure. "That'll teach you to mess with me," he said.

Moo tried to run out of the trailer in the commotion, but the man got hold of him before he could succeed. He slammed the door and locked it tight before jumping back into the driver's seat of his truck. When he drove off, he no longer meandered along the road. He peeled away and left a cloud of dust in his wake.

Missy and Ruthie could hear Moo crying out for help as the truck sped down the road. They glanced at each other and, in a split second, knew what they had to do.

The cat and dog took off running after the truck. Ruthie reached it first and leapt at the door, holding on to the handle with all four paws. Missy came right behind her. She couldn't fit on the door, but ran to the front of the trailer and managed to jump onto the hitch between the trailer and the truck.

The two frightened animals held on for their lives as the truck speeded up and left the sanctuary far behind.

*

Ruthie felt the truck slowing down and relaxed her grip on the door handle. The truck made a right turn, and she saw that they were turning into a gas station. If they had any chance at all of getting out of this situation, this was it.

A car crossed the truck's path, forcing the evil man in the cowboy hat to slam on the truck's brakes. Ruthie just barely managed to hang on with one paw, and cringed as she heard Missy yelp in pain. Clearly the dog had fallen off the truck.

Ruthie would tend to Missy later. Now, as the truck slowed to a stop beside a gas pump, she knew she had to get the trailer door open so Moo could get out. She balanced herself with her back paws and worked on the handle with her front. She knew she had it, but waited for the man to go inside to pay for his gas before she made her move.

The cat pulled on the handle and tumbled onto the parking lot as the door opened. Moo's brown eyes widened when he saw his friend on the concrete below him.

"Ruthie?"

"Get out of there, Moo. Hurry!"

Moo didn't argue and ran out of the trailer.

Ruthie pointed her paw towards the back of the gas station. "Hide over there," she said. "You need to hide before he comes back out."

"How did you...."

"Hurry!" Ruthie hissed.

Confused, Moo did as he was told. To Ruthie's immense relief, he made it behind the building just before the man walked out the door of the station. Now Ruthie was the one who needed to hurry.

She jumped up and pushed the door of the trailer closed, then darted towards the grass that lined the station driveway. She made it to Missy, who was lying still on her side, before the man even got back to the door of his truck.

Ruthie was overcome with relief when she saw Missy getting up from the grass. She had been terrified that the dog was unconscious or worse.

"Are you okay, Missy?"

Missy winced as she tried to stand. "I think my leg is broken," she said.

Sure enough, her right front leg dangled uselessly at her side.

"Oh no. We need to get you help."

"It hurts really bad, Ruthie." Missy had started to shake from both fear and pain.

"I know. But we need to get out of here before we can do anything about that."

The cat glanced around the parking lot. Fortunately, none of the people seemed to notice the dog and cat sitting in the grass near the entrance. She knew it was a safe bet that Moo was the only one who would attract attention.

"Listen, Missy. Moo is over there behind the station. I know it hurts but I need you to hobble over there with me. We need to get out of here together so we can get help. Can you make it? You can lean on me."

Missy licked her lips and yawned repeatedly to calm herself. She leaned against her friend and managed to stand on three legs. "I can make it," she said.

They hobbled through the grass and made it to where Moo waited.

"Missy!" he cried. "What happened to you?"

"I fell off the truck when it stopped to come in here. I broke my leg."

"Oh, Missy. I'm sorry!"

"Hush, both of you," Ruthie said. "We don't have time to talk right now."

She knew luck was in their favor, as the sun was rapidly setting and soon they would be able to move under cover of darkness. Just what they needed.

"Moo, you're going to need to carry Missy. She can't walk on her own."

Moo lay down on the grass and got as low as he could so that Missy could climb onto his back. She yelped in pain when her injured leg touched Moo's skin, but she made it. Moo stood up as slowly and with as much gentleness as he could. The two looked to Ruthie for what to do next.

The cat had walked into the grass away from the station, her mouth open and her nostrils twitching as she picked up the various scents around them.

"Good news," she said when she returned. "I recognize the smell of a place and I don't think it's too far. We can get help."

Ruthie didn't give her friends a chance to respond. "Follow me," she said, and headed east through the grass. She was sure that no one had seen their little party leave the gas station.

She was wrong.

A pair of eyes watched the trio of animals walk away from the station from a nearby tree. Their owner jumped to the ground and followed behind.

*

Ruthie wanted to walk more quickly, in fact she wanted to run at full feline speed, but she knew that their trek had to be slow-going with Missy perched so perilously on Moo's back. Missy was trying her best to be strong and unafraid, but every so often Ruthie heard her whimpers of pain. Besides that, the trio walked in silence, not wanting to make any noise that could draw attention to their unusual group. The moon had come out now, bright and full in the dark sky. Ruthie considered it a good omen. She was beginning to feel more and more confident that they really were going to get through this journey without any more trouble.

"Guys? Hey, guys? Guys, wait up! Hey! Wait up!"

Ruthie and Moo both froze at the sound of the high-pitched, squealing voice that broke their silence. They turned around, Ruthie's back already arched.

"Hey, you heard me! Great, great!"

"Oh boy," Moo said. "A squirrel? Seriously?"

Yes, it was a squirrel. As the little animal ran to them, Ruthie hissed and pinned back her ears.

The squirrel stopped. "Hey, hey, calm down, okay? I don't want any trouble with you, cat."

He stood on his back legs in a defensive posture, his tail bushy and erect. The squirrel wiggled his torso in a move obviously meant to intimidate.

Ruthie burst out laughing and let down her guard. "Are you trying to scare me, squirrel? Really? Stop the nonsense and tell us what you want."

The squirrel relaxed his posture and returned all four legs to the ground. He ran in a circle around the group before answering. It seemed nearly impossible for him to remain still.

"I saw you leave the gas station back there and I followed," he said. "I thought I recognized you. Don't you live at Sunrise?"

"How do you know that?" Moo asked.

"I was born there. Grew up there too. And my sisters still live there. My name's Bobby. Well, Bobby the 3rd, actually. My dad was Bobby, and his dad before him too. All named Bobby. Yep."

"So what are you doing here, Bobby? Why aren't you at Sunrise?" Ruthie asked.

"I decided to move to the city once I got older. Figured it would be more exciting out here."

Bobby once again ran a lap around the Sunrise trio. He picked up a nut and began to furiously chew it.

Moo hung his head. "That's what I thought too. I guess I wasn't wrong. It is exciting outside of Sunrise. But not in a good way."

"You don't think so? I love it here. Yep, love it. Love it."

Bobby talked nearly as quickly as he ran, and Ruthie found herself immensely irritated by his constant movement. She flicked her whiskers, desperate to chase this pest and stop his chattering. But she restrained herself. She didn't have time for those sorts of games right now.

"Well, Bobby," she said, "we need to get moving. As you can see, our friend Missy here needs help."

"Are you going back to Sunrise? Are you? If so, can you tell my sisters I said hi? And my nieces and nephews too? Tell them I'll get back to visit soon enough."

"We'll tell them," Moo said, not bothering to try to figure out how they would know which of the many squirrels around the farm were related to Bobby. Maybe they all were.

"Great, great. I sure do appreciate it. Yep, I do."

"Goodbye then, Bobby," Ruthie said.

"Goodbye now. And thank you. Thank you much. Good luck to you!"

The squirrel made one more lap around the animals, then took off in a flash towards the nearest tree. He was up the tree and out of sight with one dizzying leap.

"Let's hope that's the last pest we encounter," Ruthie said, once again opening her mouth and flaring her nostrils to pick up the scent she wanted. "We don't need any more interruptions."

"Have you guys ever talked to the squirrels around the farm?" Missy asked. "I haven't."

"No," Ruthie answered. "They've always kept to themselves. I wish this one had continued to do so."

Moo chuckled. "You didn't like Bobby, son of Bobby, grandson of Bobby, Ruthie?"

Ruthie scowled and ignored the question as they resumed their trek.

"I'm sorry I got you guys in so much trouble," Moo said. "And I'm sorry I got you hurt, Missy."

Neither Missy nor Ruthie responded.

"I know I was stupid," Moo said. "As dumb as that dumb squirrel Bobby."

"That you were, Moo," Ruthie said.

"You should have listened to us and stayed at home," Missy said.

"I know." Moo hung his head down in shame.

"But I accept your apology," Missy said.

Moo's ears perked up.

"I do too. We all do dumb things sometimes." Ruthie stopped in her tracks and opened her mouth to get a good sniff and make sure they were still heading in the right direction. Satisfied, she continued on. "Well, except for me. I don't do dumb things. In general, cats don't."

"Oh, boy," Missy and Moo said in unison.

"The truth hurts, my friends."

Moo chuckled. "I love you guys," he said. "You're the best."

"We love you too, Moo," Missy said from his back. "That's why we wanted you to stay home with us."

"I wonder if we'll ever see home again," Moo said, tears forming at the corners of his big brown eyes.

"Of course we will," Ruthie hissed. "Both of you be quiet and let me concentrate. I'll get us home."

None of the animals realized another pair of eyes was now watching them. Big yellow eyes. The eyes of a much bigger animal.

*

In spite of his friends' earlier insistence that Moo couldn't sing, he couldn't help doing so now. It was an activity that always helped him to calm down. He hoped maybe it would do the same for his friends as they all continued their journey.

"Should auld acquaintance be forgot, And never brought to mind.."

"Why are you singing a New Year's Eve song, Moo?" Missy asked.

Moo shrugged his shoulders. "I don't know. It just popped into my head. I guess I was thinking about the New Year's Eve party Mom had last year. Remember?"

"Yeah, I remember," Missy said.

Lots of friends had come to the farm that night and everyone had been so happy and having fun. It felt a long way off now.

"Should auld acquaintance be forgot, And days o' lang syne!"

The animals were passing through Dublin, Ohio, following Ruthie back to Marysville. Or at least to the place she said they could get help getting back to Marysville. They passed numerous houses with their lights on and could look through the windows to see families gathered together enjoying their evening. Dogs barked at them and Missy translated what was said. In each case, the dogs were simply warning the group to not get any closer to their homes and families.

Sometimes, Missy barked a reply to assure the dogs they had no intention of disrespecting their territory, but mostly she was too tired and in too much pain to bother. The dogs quieted as soon as they'd passed anyway.

Moo continued his melancholy song.

"For auld lang syne, my dear, For auld lang..."

And stopped in mid-line when the smell of a predator overwhelmed all of their senses. Before any of them could figure out where the scent was coming from, a coyote jumped out of the bushes to their left and blocked their path.

All three animals froze. Missy screamed in fright.

The coyote had huge yellow eyes that gleamed with hatred and hunger. His fur was raised along his back, enhancing his already large appearance. A drop of saliva dripped from his exposed fang.

"What a strange little crowd I've run into," he said, licking his lips with anticipation.

Ruthie arched her back and let out a menacing, low throated growl. The coyote started towards her, and she jumped on Moo's back.

The coyote closed in on Moo, ignoring Missy's ferocious barking and Ruthie's continued growls.

"I've never tasted a cow before," the coyote said. "This is my lucky night."

"Get away from us or I'll kick you," Moo said. He slammed a hoof on the ground to emphasize his threat.

"Will you really then?"

Moo tried to ignore the laughing yellow eyes of the coyote. He didn't know when he'd ever been more scared.

"I'm not scared of you, coyote," he said, hoping he sounded convincing. "Don't make me kick you. You'll regret it."

The coyote glanced at Moo's hoof and took a few steps back. Moo got the impression that perhaps he'd been kicked before. If so, it was Moo's lucky night instead of his.

"That's right, get back and leave us alone." Moo stamped the ground and flung his hoof towards the coyote. This time there was no doubt the animal jumped back in fear. The coyote raised his haunches and lowered his belly to the ground.

"Okay, okay," he said. "I was just trying to scare you. You don't have to go crazy trying to kick me."

"You weren't just trying to scare us."

"Sure I was! Geez."

Moo, Ruthie and Missy all stared at the coyote with disgust.

"Oh okay, okay. But give me a break, will you? A coyote has to eat you know."

"Just get away from us, coyote," Moo said. "Go find something else to eat."

The coyote stayed low to the ground and disappeared into the bushes. All three animals let out sighs of relief.

"Boy, that was close," Missy said. "What next?"

"Home, that's what's next," Ruthie said. She jumped from Moo's back and took her place in front of him. "Let's get going. And Moo, please, no more singing."

"I agree with that! No more singing, Moo. Really."

"You guys are no fun," Moo said. "No fun at all."

*

Leaving the homes and families of Dublin behind, Moo and Ruthie walked more quickly, anxious to get to their destination without running into any more menaces. As they drew closer to a building in the distance, Missy lifted her head from Moo's back and sniffed the air around her.

"I know where you're taking us, Ruthie. I smell it too."

"Where? What do you smell?" Moo asked.

"The vet's office."

"The vet? How could you find the vet?"

"Because I have a nose," Ruthie said. "If Missy hadn't been hurt and distracted, she would have smelled it earlier too. Our friends aren't far now."

"I don't know if I've ever thought of the vets as my friends."

Ruthie scowled. "You will now, Moo. Or at least I hope so. I hope they will help us."

She stopped at the edge of a driveway and nodded in the direction of a large one-story red brick building. White pillars led to its front door.

"Here we are," she said, reading the sign next to them. "The Ohio State University Veterinary Medical Center, Dublin. Missy and I have both been here."

"I never have," Moo said. "Do they help cows?"

"No, just small animals like us. But you don't need medical help, do you? Missy does. They will help her and then they can help us get home. They know Mom."

"You're so smart, Ruthie," Moo said.

"I know I am. Now let's go and everybody keep your paws and hooves crossed that they recognize us."

The cat started up the driveway. Moo and Missy followed behind, and Ruthie could hear Missy panting from both pain and anxiety.

"What are we going to do if they don't recognize us?" Missy asked.

"We shouldn't worry about that until it happens, Missy," Moo replied. "And it won't happen. They'll know you guys."

Ruthie remained quiet. She wasn't as confident as Moo about that.

They got to the door and Ruthie jumped up to paw at the bell. After a few tries, they heard it ring.

A woman came to the door and looked startled when she saw the cow, dog, and cat staring back at her.

"What on earth?" She stepped out and looked around, obviously looking for human companions to the animals in front of her. When she didn't find any, she turned back to the door and called for another woman named Veronica to come join her.

Missy's ears perked up at that name. She had met a Veronica here more than once. And if she remembered right, Veronica also came out to the farm sometimes with the vets who cared for the big animals like Moo.

"Oh please, oh please," she whispered into Moo's thick fur.

"What is it?" the woman named Veronica asked.

"There are three animals out here and I don't see any people with them. But the doorbell rang."

Veronica walked out with a puzzled expression and Missy yipped with joy when she saw her. Veronica. She knew Veronica!

"Oh my goodness," Veronica said. "What is going on here?" She looked from Ruthie to Moo to Missy and back again.

"Missy, is that you?"

Missy wagged her tail and barked in response. She tried to wiggle and nearly fell off Moo's back. Veronica came towards her as she whimpered in pain.

"What's the matter, sweetie?" Veronica saw the dog's mangled leg and grimaced. "Oh no. We need to get you inside."

As soon as he heard her voice, Moo realized he also knew Veronica. She came to the farm sometimes when Moo or Wesley or one of the horses needed medical care. He thought she was one of the vet's helpers. Now, he let out a loud moo in the hopes that she would recognize him, too.

Veronica jumped as if she had almost forgotten that Missy was resting on top of a cow.

"Calm down, buddy," she said. "It's okay." She reached for Moo's head and her hand stopped in mid-air. "Wait a minute. Moo? Baby Moo? It's you, isn't it?"

Moo bellowed as loudly as he could and stomped his front hoof on the pavement.

At that, Ruthie came and jumped on Moo's back as well. She didn't think Veronica knew her, as she didn't recognize Veronica, but she wanted to make sure the vets knew she was here too.

"You obviously know these animals," the woman who had first answered the door said.

"I do and it's the craziest thing. They live at Sunrise Sanctuary in Marysville. I can't imagine how they got here."

Ruthie purred and nuzzled her face against Veronica's hand.

"I don't think I know you, kitty, but are you from Sunrise too? You must be."

Veronica rubbed her hands on her scrubs and grabbed Moo's bridle. "We need to get you guys inside and get Missy some help from Dr. Matthews. We don't really have a space big enough for you Moo but we'll work something out until your mom can get here. I'm going to call her right away."

Moo walked through the door of the veterinary hospital with Ruthie and Missy on his back. His eyes had filled with tears when he heard Veronica say she was calling mom. Mom would come get them and everything would be okay. She would bring them home. Moo was going to go home!

*

"Cock-a-doodle-do! Cock-a-doodle-do!"

Mr. Big announced the arrival of another day at Sunrise Sanctuary. Moo was so sleepy he could barely open his eyes. He and Ruthie and Missy hadn't arrived back home until close to three in the morning. And now Mr. Big was already yelling and making noise just a few hours later.

Moo sighed and stomped his hooves to try to wake up.

"Be quiet," Ruthie said from her favorite corner. "I'm trying to sleep. Thanks to you I didn't get any sleep last night."

"You think I did?"

"Well you didn't deserve any sleep. You caused the whole mess!"

Moo chuckled. It was true, and he had a feeling Ruthie wasn't going to let him forget it any time soon.

Moo didn't think his mom would let him forget it either, even though she had no idea how it had all come about. But he'd never forget the look on her face when she'd run into the veterinary hospital and seen Moo, Ruthie, and Missy. Moo had expected her to yell at them but instead she'd burst into tears and given them all hugs.

"Thank God," she'd kept whispering as she hugged and kissed each one over and over. His mom had cried so much he'd started crying. And he was fairly sure Ruthie had too, although she'd never admit it.

They waited while the doctor put Missy's leg in a cast and gave her medicine for the pain, then they'd all piled in to Mom's truck and trailer and headed back to Sunrise. Moo had cried again when they'd pulled into their driveway and he'd seen his barn.

"Cock-a-doodle-do! Cock-a-doodle-do!"

Mr. Big's alerts spread throughout the farm and Moo heard his friends all getting ready to start their day. Another day was here whether Moo was ready for it or not. He yawned and closed his eyes, shaking his head back and forth to try and wake up.

When he opened his eyes, he saw that he had company. Baby Nathan the pig stepped tentatively into the barn.

"Welcome back, Moo," the piglet said.

"Thanks."

"I was really scared when I saw you get put on that truck. I got put on a truck once and it was the scariest thing ever until I ended up here."

"I know, Nathan. I remember."

"Were you scared on that truck?"

"Yes I was."

"I'm glad Ruthie and Missy helped you get out of it."

Moo felt tears coming to his eyes again and fought them off. He had to remember he wasn't a baby anymore like Nathan was. Enough of this crying.

"I'm glad too."

The piglet looked up at Moo with reverence. "I'm glad you're back. The farm wouldn't have been the same without you. I'd miss your singing."

This time, Moo couldn't stop the tears. "Thanks, Nathan. I think you're the only one who feels that way."

"Cock-a-doodle-do! Cock-a-doodle-do!"

Nathan jumped at Mr. Big's cry. "I guess it's time for breakfast!" he said, and ran out of the barn. Meal time was Nathan's favorite time of the day.

"I guess it's my favorite time too," Moo said, mostly to himself since he knew Ruthie was trying to sleep.

Moo let out a sigh and started to leave the barn so he could get in on the morning serving of hay. He glanced at the cross-stitch sign on the side of the barn, the one Ruthie had read to him back when he'd first moved in.

"Be it ever so humble, there's no place like home," he sung softly.

Home, sweet home.

About the author:

Julie Flanders is a librarian by day and a writer all the rest of
the time. She is an animal lover and has written numerous
features about pets and the importance of animal rescue for a
variety of media outlets. Julie's novels include the paranormal
thrillers Polar Night and Polar Day as well as the historical
mystery The Ghosts of Aquinnah. She is also the author of the
horror novella The Turnagain Arm. Baby Moo's Great Escape
is her first book for children.

Find Julie at www.julieflanders.net or on Twitter at
@JulesFlanders